DISNEY'S
THE LITTLE MERMAID
SPECIAL EDITION

Adapted by **Michael Teitelbaum**

Illustrated by **Sue DiCicco**

A GOLDEN BOOK • NEW YORK

Copyright © 1999, 2006 Disney Enterprises, Inc. All rights reserved.
Published in the United States by Golden Books, an imprint of Random House Children's Books,
a division of Random House, Inc., New York, in conjunction with Disney Enterprises, Inc. Originally published by
Golden Books, a division of Random House, Inc., in 1999. Golden Books, A Golden Book, A Little Golden Book,
the G colophon, and the distinctive gold spine are registered trademarks of Random House, Inc.

www.goldenbooks.com
www.randomhouse.com/kids/disney
Library of Congress Control Number: 2003100639
ISBN-13: 978-0-7364-2177-5
ISBN-10: 0-7364-2177-7
Printed in the United States of America
30 29 28 27 26 25 24 23 22

King Triton, the great sea king, had many daughters who loved the undersea world.

But Triton's youngest daughter, Ariel, dreamed of the world above the water's surface—the world of humans.

Ariel and her friend Flounder liked to go to the surface to visit Scuttle the seagull. Scuttle told them all about the humans' objects that Ariel found at the bottom of the sea.

One day Triton learned about Ariel's trips to the surface. The sea king grew very angry. He asked his friend Sebastian the crab to keep an eye on Ariel.

A few days later, Ariel noticed a ship sailing way up on the surface of the water. She quickly swam toward it. "Ariel! Ariel! Please come back!" cried Sebastian as he and Flounder swam after her.

When Ariel surfaced, she saw a huge ship filled with sailors. Ariel's eyes lit up when she spotted the sailor the others called Prince Eric. It was love at first sight!

Suddenly the sky darkened. Heavy rain began to fall, and lightning split the sky. The ship was tossed on the waves, and the prince was thrown overboard!

"I've got to save him!" thought Ariel. She grabbed the drowning prince and swam to shore, pulling him onto the beach. Prince Eric did not stir as Ariel gently touched his face and sang him a love song.

Soon Ariel heard the prince's crew searching for him. She did not want to be seen by the humans, so she kissed the prince and dove back into the sea.

Prince Eric awoke to find Sir Grimsby, his loyal steward, at his side. Sir Grimsby was happy that Eric was alive.

"A girl . . . rescued me," said the prince. "She was singing. She had the most beautiful voice."

Prince Eric, too, had fallen in love.

King Triton was furious when he discovered that Ariel had fallen in love with a human. He rushed to the grotto where Ariel kept her collection of humans' treasures.

"Contact between the human world and the merworld is strictly forbidden!" Triton shouted.

He raised his magic trident and fired bolts of energy around the cave, destroying the treasures. Then the mighty sea king left.

Ariel buried her face in her hands and began to cry.

Meanwhile, not far away, evil forces were at work in the undersea kingdom. Ursula, the sea witch, who had tried once before to overthrow Triton, was looking for a way to take over. Through her crystal ball she could see Ariel crying, and an idea came to her.

Ursula sent her slimy eel servants, Flotsam and Jetsam, to Ariel's grotto. There they convinced the Little Mermaid that Ursula could help her to get her beloved prince. Ariel was so upset that she ignored Sebastian's warnings and swam off with Flotsam and Jetsam to meet with the sea witch.

"My dear," said the witch. "Here's the deal. I'll make a potion that will turn you into a human for three days. Before the sun sets on the third day, you've got to get dear old princie to kiss you. If he kisses you, you'll remain human permanently. But if he doesn't, you turn back into a mermaid and you belong to me!"

In return for the potion, the witch wanted Ariel's voice.

"My voice?" asked Ariel. "Without my voice, how can I—"

"You'll still have your looks, your pretty face," replied Ursula.

After Ariel agreed to Ursula's deal, an amazing change took place. Ariel's voice flew from her body and was captured in a seashell around Ursula's neck. Ariel lost her tail, grew legs, and became a human.

When Ariel went in search of the prince, she was helped ashore by her friends. She tried to speak to them, but no sound came out.

A short while later, Ariel saw Prince Eric. The prince had been lovesick ever since hearing her sing. At first the prince thought Ariel was the girl who had rescued him. But when he learned that she couldn't speak, he knew he was wrong.

Prince Eric felt sorry for Ariel. She needed a place to stay, so he took her back to his palace.

Over the next two days, Prince Eric grew to like Ariel more and more. During a romantic boat ride, Eric was about to kiss Ariel when Flotsam and Jetsam overturned the boat.

"That was a close one. Too close," said Ursula, who was watching in her crystal ball. "It's time Ursula took matters into her own tentacles." The sea witch mixed a magic potion and changed herself into a beautiful young maiden.

On the morning of the third day, there was great excitement throughout the kingdom. Prince Eric was going to marry a young maiden he had just met!

Ursula, disguised as the maiden, had used Ariel's voice to trick Eric. He now believed that the maiden was the girl who had saved him from the shipwreck.

Poor Ariel was heartbroken.

The wedding ceremony was to take place on Prince
Eric's new boat. Scuttle flew by just as the bride
passed in front of a mirror. Her reflection was that of
the sea witch! Scuttle rushed off to tell Ariel and the
rest of his friends.

Sebastian quickly formed a plan. Flounder helped
Ariel get out to Eric's ship. Scuttle arranged for some
of his seagull friends to delay the wedding. And
Sebastian hurried to find King Triton.

Prince Eric and the maiden were about to be married when a flock of seagulls, led by Scuttle, swooped down on the bride. She screamed in the sea witch's voice.

Scuttle knocked the seashell containing Ariel's voice from around the maiden's neck. The shell shattered, and Ariel's voice returned to her.

"It was you all the time!" said Prince Eric.

"Oh, Eric, I wanted to tell you," said Ariel.

The sun disappeared over the horizon just as they were about to kiss. Ariel's three days were up. She changed back into a mermaid. Ursula grabbed Ariel and dove off the ship.

Thanks to Sebastian's warning, Triton was waiting for them at Ursula's lair. "I might be willing to make an exchange for someone better," cried Ursula. Triton agreed, and he became Ursula's prisoner. She now had his magic trident and control of the undersea kingdom.

All of a sudden a harpoon struck Ursula in the shoulder. Prince Eric had come to Ariel's rescue! Together they swam to the surface.

Ursula followed close behind them, and she grew bigger and bigger with anger, until she rose out of the water.

Prince Eric swam to his ship and climbed on board. He grabbed the wheel and turned the ship toward Ursula. Just as the sea witch was about to fire a deadly bolt at Ariel from the trident, the prince's ship slammed into Ursula. The evil witch was destroyed!